The Diary

of

Robin's Toys

Ken and Angie Lake

1

Carla the Cow

Published by Sweet Cherry Publishing Limited
53 St. Stephens Road,
Leicester, LE2 1GH
United Kingdom

First Published in the UK in 2013

ISBN: 978-1-78226-029-5
Text: © Ken and Angie Lake 2013
Illustrations: (c) Vishnu Madhav and Joyson Loitongbam,
Creative Books

Title: Carla the Cow - The Diaries of Robin's Toys

Printed and Bound By Nutech Print Services, India

Every Toy Has a Story to Tell

Have you ever seen an old toy, perhaps in a cupboard, or in the attic or loft? Have you ever seen how sad they look at car boot sales, unwanted and unloved? Well, look at them closely, because every toy has a story to tell, and the older, the more decrepit, the more scruffy, the more tatty the toy is, the more interesting its story could be. Here are just a few of those toys and their stories.

7th October, 09.15

It was Sunday morning again. Robin had finished his breakfast and was waiting for Grandad to arrive to take him to the car boot sale.

So he opened the curtains to look down the street. *How strange,* he thought. He couldn't see anything. Had the street disappeared?

Outside, it was grey and dull; a very thick fog had developed during the night.

As he peered out, he could just make out a car's headlamps. The car was travelling at a walking pace, hardly moving. Robin could see the fog and it was almost still; he just saw a bit of a swirl as the car passed by.

Mum had the radio playing in the kitchen, and somebody was singing, "*I can see clearly now ...*" *Can you really?* thought Robin as he stared out of the window at the thick fog. *I wish I could.*

He stared down the street again, and although he could see very little through the dull gloom, something was moving. It had a strange shape. He counted the legs. Six? What on earth had six legs? Was it a monster? This was like a scene from a horror movie. What could this monster be, and was it dangerous?

As the six-legged monster got near to Robin's window, he could make out what it was. *Ah, that's a relief,* he thought. It was old Mrs Woodhouse walking her big, fat dog, Wobbler.

Robin smiled to himself.
Then he thought he saw two
car headlights glowing in the
dull morning. The lights pulled
up just in front of his house.

Beep, beep! Beep, beep!

"Come on, Robin, it's Sunday morning. Time to go to the car boot sale. Come on."

It was Grandad.

Yes! This was the moment
Robin had been waiting for. He
put away his drawing pad and
ran to the front door.

"Bye, Mum. See you later."

"Okay, Robin. Take care of Grandad, and don't let him get into any trouble."

Robin laughed.

"Wow, Grandad, I didn't expect to see you this morning. The weather is so bad."

"Don't worry, Robin, it would have to be far worse than this for me to miss my favourite day of the week."

Grandad drove carefully and slowly because it was difficult to see very far ahead. When they arrived at the car boot sale, it was still very dull. There were a few stalls, but not many people.

"Okay, Robin, here is your 50 pence. Let's see what we can find."

"Thank you, Grandad. I can't see many of the usual stallholders; they obviously haven't come because of the foggy weather."

Nelly Knitwear had shown up as usual.

"Good morning, Mrs Knitwear," Grandad said. "That's a lovely bobble hat you're making."

Nelly looked up at Grandad with a very cross expression and answered in a very snooty voice,

"Put your glasses on, Harry Smith. Anyone can see that it's not a bobble hat."

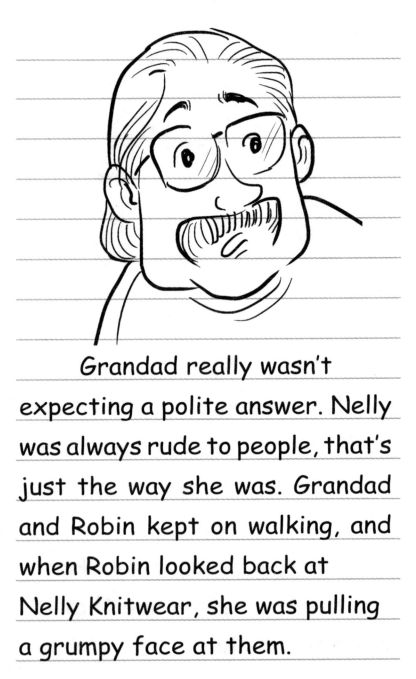

Grandad really wasn't expecting a polite answer. Nelly was always rude to people, that's just the way she was. Grandad and Robin kept on walking, and when Robin looked back at Nelly Knitwear, she was pulling a grumpy face at them.

He nudged Grandad, who also looked back at Nelly Knitwear's grumpy face.

"Well, Robin, that's the best I've seen her look for weeks."

Grandad stopped to say
hello to Freddy Green-Fingers
on the plant stall.

"Good morning, Freddy."

"Good morning, Harry."

"Have you seen Nelly Knitwear this morning? She seems in a bit of a bad mood again today."

"Oh, Harry, take no notice," replied Freddy. "She's been a bit lonely since her sister left."

"I didn't know she had a sister," said Grandad.

"Oh yes. They had a little wool shop in town. It was called *Nelly and Nancy's Knitting.*

"Nelly thought that Nancy would always be there, so she didn't make any friends. Then one day, a new wool supplier called William Jones visited the shop.

"Nancy and William started talking about their interest in wool, and the next thing you knew, they were engaged.

"Then Nancy married Mr Jones and moved away to help him run his business, *William's Wool Warehouse,* in Wales.

"After that, Nelly couldn't cope on her own, so she sold the shop, and now she just knits at home and sells it at the car boot sale.

"She hardly talks to anyone and prefers her own company, but I think deep down she would like some friends."

Grandad looked at Freddy with his thoughtful face and said, "Really, Freddy? I had no idea. I'll try to be a bit more understanding next time I see her. We must be off now to find Robin a toy. I'll see you later, Freddy."

Even though the fog had lifted, it really wasn't the best day to be looking for toys at the car boot sale, but Grandad was still his normal happy self.

"Don't worry, Robin, I have a feeling that today we will find a special toy, one with a very different story."

They both wandered around in the gloom until they came to a stall called *Pete's Treats*.

His stall had lots of
computer games and lots of
baby toys, and of course lots of

baby clothes. But right at the back, in the corner, Robin spotted something unusual. It was a toy cow.

Now, as you know, most toys have happy smiley faces - that's what children like - but this cow had a long sad face. She did not look happy at all.

"Grandad, have you seen the sad-looking cow?"

"Yes, Robin, I have."

"Do you think that she has an interesting story to tell us?"

"I don't know, but if you wait a minute I will have a quick word with her."

Grandad went into a trance and mumbled something. Then he turned to Robin.

"Oh yes, I can tell that she has a lot to say, and I know we will find it very interesting."

So Robin reached into his pocket.

"Err, excuse me, Mr Treats, that cow looks interesting. How much is she?"

"Ah yes! Carla the toy cow.
Well, she is interesting in a
strange sort of way, but she is
not a very happy cow."

"Yes, I can see that, but
how much do you want for her?"

"She is so moody that I didn't really think anyone would want to buy her."

"Alright, I will give you 50 pence for her! Is that enough?"

"50 pence? Oh yes, that's alright. Thank you, young man. Shall I put Carla in a bag for you?"

"Right," said Grandad, "now let's find something for your grandma."

"What shall we get her, Grandad?"

"I know! Roses; your grandma loves roses!" he said, and dashed off to Freddy Green-Fingers' stall.

On the way home, the fog lifted, and as they turned into Grandad's street it was almost clear.

Inside, Grandma was waiting with a freshly baked Victoria sponge.

"Hello, boys," she said as they walked into the kitchen.

"Hello, Mabel. You'll never guess what I've brought you. I know how you love roses, so... well, just go and have a look in the car."

Grandma was getting really excited as she followed Robin and Grandad outside, but then her expression changed.

"Harry Smith, I don't know what to say."

There, in the back of the car, was a big sack of steaming horse manure.

"Now you can grow all the roses you want," said Grandad with a big smile.

Grandma gave him one of her looks; you know, the sort that would frighten a fierce lion. She let out a loud sigh and reached for her long broom. Grandad thought that she was going to hit him with it.

"Harry, I find my present of a bag of horse manure quite insulting. If that's what you think of me, you can take it back!"

"Take it back? Oh alright, dear."

As Grandma was armed with her long broom, this was not the best time to argue with her.

"Harry! " she shouted in her angry voice while holding her nose. "I am going out. Get rid of that ... before I get back. And enjoy the wonderful sponge cake I have made for you!"

She was not a happy
Grandma, and with that she
jumped onto her old bicycle
and stormed off down the
street.

"Okay, Grandad, we had better get rid of that horse manure before Grandma gets back."

"Yes, I agree, Robin, but first things first."

Robin and Grandad headed back to the kitchen. They cut some slices of cake, and put Carla on the kitchen table. Then Grandad cast his secret spell.

"Little toy, hear this rhyme,
Let it take you back in time,
Tales of sadness or of glory,
Little toy, reveal your story."

Carla blinked, stretched and let out a little Moooo.

"Who are you?" she asked.

"My name is Robin, and this is my grandad."

"Oh, my name is Carla. I am a cow."

"Yes, we know that, but we were wondering if you have an interesting story to tell us."

"Interesting story? Well yes, I may have. But first I am hungry. Can you offer me something to eat please?"

"Yes, alright. Would you like a slice of cake?"

"*Not at the moment, thank you, I am off cake. My favourite food is long, lush grass. Do you have any?*"

"Come on, Robin, let's go into the garden and get her some."

They came back with a big bowl full of grass, and Carla sat there chewing slowly until she was ready to tell them her story.

"Alright, if you two are sitting comfortably, let me tell you something about cows."

She paused for a while and then chewed some more grass.

"Do you know that in India cows are sacred?"

"Yes, actually, Carla, we do know that."

"I suppose you also know that we are cattle?"

"Yes, we know that as well."

"Oh, you two think you are so clever. That's it! I am not telling you any more."

Then she started to sulk.

"Oh, come on, Carla, don't be like that. Why don't you tell us something about yourself?"

"Only if you promise not to know it already."

"Yes, alright, Carla, we promise."

Robin whispered to Grandad, "I know Mr Treats said that she was moody, but I didn't know she would be this bad."

"Alright then, but I don't want you to think that cows just laze around mooing and eating grass all day long.

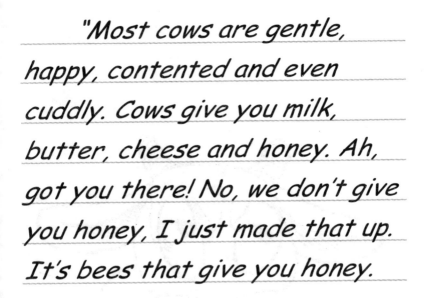

"*Most cows are gentle, happy, contented and even cuddly. Cows give you milk, butter, cheese and honey. Ah, got you there! No, we don't give you honey, I just made that up. It's bees that give you honey.*

"So, I can hear you asking, was I a typical happy cow? Well, I am going to be very honest with you both. No, I was not. I must admit that the other animals found me grumpy, bad mannered, bad tempered, selfish and rude. They even say that I was not a nice cow to be around.

"I never realised that I was such a grump. You see, I had been a dairy cow on a really big dairy farm for much of my life, and I spent a lot of time on my own.

"I had convinced myself that there wasn't really much time for making friends. Then, after a few years, I was sold to a small local farm with just a few other animals.

"I was very nervous about the move; I'd only ever known

the big unfriendly dairy farm.
On the day I arrived, some of
the animals came over to talk to
me, to welcome me and to show
me around.

"I told them that my old farm was much better, the milking machines were newer and there were more men to look after us. At the time I didn't understand, but it must have sounded like I was putting their farm down and showing off.

"They all got upset, but I didn't know what to do or say to make things better, and I quickly got known for being snooty. It wasn't long before I started to moan about everything.

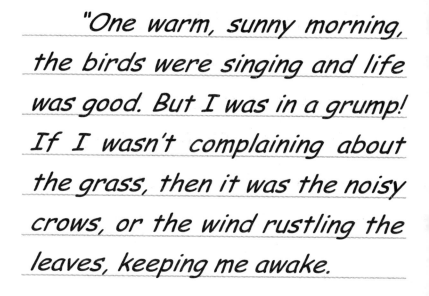

"One warm, sunny morning, the birds were singing and life was good. But I was in a grump! If I wasn't complaining about the grass, then it was the noisy crows, or the wind rustling the leaves, keeping me awake.

"The rest of the herd were totally fed up with me, they avoided me and called me Cranky Carla. They said that I was never happy, I never smiled and hated everything.

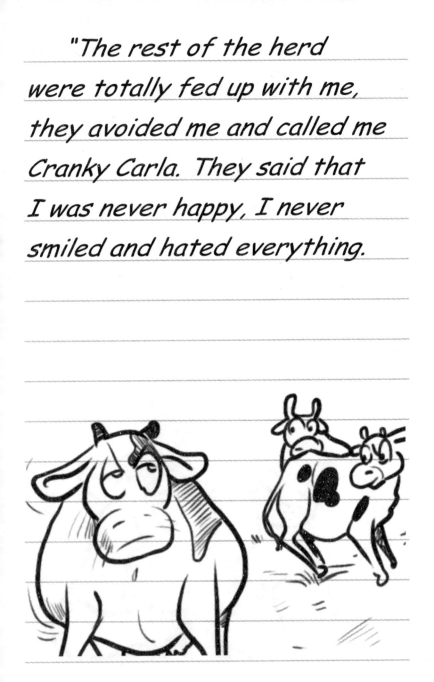

"I suppose there is a special word for cows like that; the rest of my herd called them Carlas.

"Now, every Saturday night, there was a bit of a get-together in the barn, and the girls would chew the cud about what had happened during the week.

"They would moo about this and that, play with the calves and boast about how normal they were. Secretly I always wanted to join in, but I was too proud *to tell the others how I really felt. So I just pretended that I wasn't interested and was too busy to join them.*

"Soon, every cow in the herd realised that if they moo'd at me, I would complain about something, and who needs that? Even a friendly good morning moo would get my usual response: 'What's good about it? It will be another day of standing around eating grass, moan, moan, moan.'

"I remember Carol Cow saying, 'Well, that's what you are like. You must like being miserable, complaining and being rude to everyone.'

"But let me tell you both that was not the truth. You see, I was the loneliest cow in the herd, and deep down I really did want to be popular. I needed friends, but I just didn't know how to make them and this made me very sad.

"One morning, I was alone in the far corner of the field, munching on some grass, which I had told the others I didn't like.

"I looked over the fence and saw a new herd; they must have arrived the previous night. I noticed straight away that they were Jersey cows. They had pretty light-brown coats, big, beautiful eyes and they all looked very happy.

"One of them wandered over to me."

" 'Good morning,' she said. 'My name is Charlotte. Who are you?'

"I was about to go into my 'what's good about it' speech, when I managed to stop myself from saying it. No, I thought, I can be friendly if I really try.

" 'Oh, hello, Charlotte,' I replied. 'My name is Carla.'

"We were soon mooing to each other about this and that, just like old friends. You see, if you really try, it's not difficult.

"I told Charlotte all about my problems with the rest of the herd and how lonely I was, and eventually I had to admit that it was all my fault.

" 'Well,' she said, 'you must make an effort to become popular with the others, stop complaining and do something positive.'

" 'What shall I do?' I asked.

" 'Give the rest of your herd a present,' she replied. 'A sort of peace offering.'

"I thought long and hard about this and finally came up with the ideal gift. I knew that they were bored with eating grass all the time, so I decided to make them a cake!

"I wandered all around the farm to find the ingredients, and found some nice fresh hay in the horses' stable, some carrots, some turnips and some sugar beet.

"When Saturday night came around, they were all gathered in the barn, mooing and gossiping as usual. Then I arrived with my cake, and I was very proud of it.

"All the cows were happy that I had made an effort to be popular. They made a great fuss of me and said how wonderful I was. They even called me their friend.

"The others ate most of the cake, but they left a piece for me. As I ate it, I realised that it tasted awful.

"They had eaten the cake and said that it was nice just to be polite. This taught me a very important lesson about being nice to others. I also realised that the grass didn't taste so bad after all."

"Wow, thank you, Carla, for being so honest with us. That's quite a story," said Grandad.

"Right, Grandad, we have something to do before Grandma gets back."

"What's that, Robin?"

"We have to get rid of that smelly horse manure."

"Oh yes. The car boot sale will still be open; let's take it back to Freddy Green-Fingers."

So that's what they did.

"Hello, Freddy. Mabel didn't like her rose food. Will you take it back please?"

"Alright, Harry, but I shall have to buy it back from you at a discounted price."

"Discounted price? Why is that?"

"Well, now it's second-hand horse manure."

"It was second-hand when I bought it from you; it had already had one previous owner... a horse!"

"Sorry, Harry, but that's the law."

"Whose law?"

"Mine, actually."

Grandad couldn't argue with that.

"Grandma was really cranky when she left; you had better buy her something else," Robin said.

"Yes, Robin, I am sure you are right. Now I feel sorry for Nelly Knitwear, so let's get something from her stall."

"Hello, Miss Knitwear. I would like one of those for my wife please."

Grandad pointed at what he thought was a bobble hat.

"Shall I put it in a bag for you?"

When they got back to Grandad's house, Grandma had calmed down a bit, so he gave her the new present.

"Here you are, dear, this is for you. It's for the cold weather."

"Harry, what is this?"

"Well, dear, it's a bobble hat. It's hand-made by Nelly Knitwear. Look, her card is inside."

"Why has it got holes in it?"

"Those are to put your ears through."

"If I do that, my ears will get cold."

"Well, you can also wear it when the weather is hot."

"Why would I want to wear a woolly hat when the weather is hot?"

"Just hang on, dear, give me time. I shall think of a reason soon."

"Right, I shall phone Nelly Knitwear and find out what it really is."

So that's what she did. They chatted for quite a long time, mainly about knitting and cooking.

"Harry, what you have bought me to put on my head is something to put on a teapot to keep it warm. This is not a bobble hat, it's a tea cosy!"

"Oh, very well, dear. Could we just call it a head cosy?"

After the telephone call, Grandma and Nelly became good friends. Nelly taught Grandma a lot about knitting, and Grandma taught Nelly a lot about cooking.

Then, one day, Nelly made Grandma a carrot cake for a present. Grandma introduced Nelly to some of her friends and she became a better, happier person. And it was all thanks to Grandad, a bag of smelly horse manure and a tea cosy.